Nikki & Deja

the NEWSY NEWS NEWSLETTER

by Karen English

Illustrated by Laura Freeman

sandpiper
Houghton Mifflin Harcourt
Boston ★ New York

To all the Nikkis and Dejas everywhere.
– K.E.

To my wonderful family.
– L.F.

Text copyright © 2010 by Karen English
Illustrations copyright © 2010 by Laura Freeman

All rights reserved. Published in the United States by Sandpiper,
an imprint of Houghton Mifflin Harcourt Publishing Company.
Originally published in hardcover in the United States by Clarion Books,
an imprint of Houghton Mifflin Harcourt Publishing Company, 2010.

SANDPIPER and the SANDPIPER logo are trademarks of Houghton Mifflin
Harcourt Publishing Company.

For information about permission to reproduce selections from this book,
write to Permissions, Houghton Mifflin Harcourt Publishing Company,
215 Park Avenue South, New York, New York 10003.

www.hmhbooks.com

The text of this book is set in 14-point Warnock Pro Caption.
The illustrations were executed digitally.

The Library of Congress has cataloged the hardcover edition as follows:
English, Karen.
Nikki and Deja : the newsy news newsletter / by Karen English ;
illustrated by Laura Freeman.
p. cm.
Summary: When Nikki and her best friend, Deja, start a newsletter about
what is happening on their street and in their school,
they focus more on writing exciting stories than on finding the truth.
ISBN: 978-0-547-22247-9 hardcover
ISBN: 978-0-547-40626-8 paperback
[1. Newspaper publishing—Fiction. 2. Neighborhood—Fiction.
3. Best friends—Fiction. 4. Friendship—Fiction.
5. Schools—Fiction.]
I. Freeman-Hines, Laura, ill. II. Title. III. Title: Newsy news newsletter.

PZ7.E7232Niq 2009
[Fic]—dc22   2009015845

Manufactured in the United States of America
EB 10 9 8 7 6 5 4 3 2 1
4500263590

– Contents –

1

Grab Bag

Nikki walks backwards, tilting her head way up to look directly at the sky. "Don't let me bump into anything," she says. She puts out her arms for balance. She does this kind of daredevil walk when she is feeling especially happy, especially satisfied. Deja walks alongside, watching her.

Nikki is in high spirits. She got the I Spy key chain out of Ms. Shelby's grab bag. Everyone wanted it last time, and no one picked it. Once a month, those who have stickers straight across Ms. Shelby's behavior chart get to reach into her grab bag, without looking, and pick out a prize. They have only ten seconds to take something out, during which time they have to furiously feel around for the prize they have their "eye" on, so to speak. The day before grab bag day, Ms. Shelby always lines up the prizes on her desk for a full minute so her students can memorize their shapes and sizes. Then she drops them back into the bag with a sly smile and a little chuckle.

Almost everyone—the good kids at least—had their eye on that I Spy key chain with the miniature I Spy board encased in a tiny plastic globe. Part of the globe even twists to magnify certain sections. The items to find are listed in tiny print along the bottom of the picture. You have to slide the magnifying circle over the teeny words to see what you have to "spy." It is the neatest little gadget, Nikki thinks. Everyone thought so. Everyone reached into that canvas bag with thoughts of the I Spy key chain.

Deja hadn't gotten it. She'd gotten the hole puncher in the shape of a mouse. She admitted to Nikki that she'd searched and searched for the key chain, but then the ten seconds ran out and she grabbed what was nearest her hand. What was she going to do with a stupid hole puncher? she'd asked.

Nikki spins around like a whirlybird and then stops abruptly. She's spotted Mrs. Markham. "Hi, Mrs. Markham," she says to their corner neighbor, who's all decked out in a sun hat and gardening apron. Mrs. Markham is examining the undersides of the leaves on her rosebush. Since Nikki stops, Deja has to stop, too.

"Hi, girls," Mrs. Markham says, straightening up. "Do you know that this Bermuda Mystery Rose is featured in the *Blue Island Rose Society Newsletter*?" She smiles down at them.

Nikki and Deja look at each other. They have no idea what Mrs. Markham is talking about.

"I'm pretty proud of it." She gazes at her flowers, beaming.

Nikki and Deja look at the rosebush, then back at Mrs. Markham.

"Congratulations," Nikki says finally.

"Congratulations," Deja says, following suit.

"Guess what, Mrs. Markham?" Nikki says.

"Oh, no," Deja says under her breath.

Nikki catches that, but ignores her. "I got the prize everyone wanted out of the grab bag today!"

"Say what?" Mrs. Markham asks, her eyes still on her roses.

"Ms. Shelby, our teacher . . . She has this grab bag at the end of every month—just for the good kids. You have to put your hand in without looking, and you only have ten seconds to choose something, and I got the prize *everybody* wanted!"

Mrs. Markam frowns at a leaf. "How'd you do that?"

Deja sighs heavily. Nikki has already explained her success to Ms. Shelby, and then to the custodian, and then to one of the kids in Mr. Beaumont's class who was going by to get to the school bus. She has told her story to anyone who'd listen.

"See, I knew I was only going to have ten seconds, so I thought to myself, *Just feel for the chain. Just feel for the chain.* And that's what I did. I just concentrated on feeling for the chain. I swirled my fingers all around the bottom of the bag, 'cause I had a feeling it was on the bottom. And it was! I grabbed it before Ms. Shelby said, 'Time's up!'" Nikki has worked herself up into a bundle of excitement and is now grinning broadly.

"My, my . . ." Mrs. Markham says. "Well, good for you."

Deja nudges Nikki. "Come on. I gotta get home."

They say goodbye to Mrs. Markam and continue down Fulton Street.

Nikki is quiet for a while, reliving her triumph. In a quiet voice with a secretive hush, she begins, "See I knew that the key chain—"

"You already told me," Deja says quickly.

"So? I was just saying . . ."

"But I already know how you picked it, because you've already said it a zillion times."

"Not a zillion times."

"Well, it seems like it."

"I think you're jealous because I got the I Spy key chain."

"I'm not jealous at all."

Nikki is silent. She knows she can go on—because she is right—but she chooses not to.

"You want to come in?" Nikki asks when they reach their two houses.

"Guess so." Deja follows Nikki up the front porch steps. They stop to peek into the kitchen.

Nikki's mom is peeling a potato over the sink. "Hi, girls. Nikki, you've got laundry to take up, and don't forget the towels."

"Okay, but Mom, guess what? Guess what I got!"

Deja rolls her eyes.

Nikki holds the key chain up and spins it around her finger. "This is a grab bag prize. Everybody who got to get a grab bag prize—the good kids—wanted to get this prize. But only *I* knew how to get it. I was the one who knew to feel around the bottom of the bag and only feel for the chain part . . ."

As she describes her success, Nikki catches Deja biting on her thumbnail, then looking down at her shoes. She hears Deja take a deep, slow breath and sees her press her lips together before letting it out loudly.

"Good for you," Nikki's mom says, dropping the peeled potato into a pot.

Deja follows Nikki to her room upstairs. Nikki places the key chain on her bookshelf, then starts to put away her folded laundry. She puts things away just so: socks in the sock drawer, pajamas in the pajama drawer, play clothes in the play clothes drawer. Nikki is super neat. Her closet is color-coded. Her books are alphabetized by title on her bookshelf. Nikki notices Deja looking at the bookshelf, eyeing the I Spy key chain in the center of the top shelf. She watches Deja look out the window and then back at the key chain again. Deja has a funny expression on her face. She looks as if she'd like to throw Nikki's I Spy key chain out the window.

Nikki grabs the stack of towels and heads for the linen closet in the hall. She feels Deja watching her. When Nikki comes back, she looks at her bookshelf—and her I Spy key chain. She glances at Deja. "You wanna play mancala?"

Deja shrugs. She gets up off the bed and follows Nikki downstairs and out to the porch. Nikki suspects that Deja is happy to get away from the I Spy key chain with its tiny picture of various objects and special magnifying dome.

2

Flat–Ground Ollie

The good thing about going out to the front porch is that they can just sit and watch their neighborhood. There is always something to see on Fulton Street. Now there is something interesting going on in front of Darnell Woolsy's house. Nikki and Deja sit down on the steps and open the wooden mancala board, then pause to see what is happening.

Darnell is one of the bigger boys, in the fifth grade at Carver Elementary. He and Evan Richardson, who lives around the corner, are carrying plastic crates from Darnell's garage to the walkway in front of his house. They set them down and begin to arrange them, one in front of the other—close together, but with spaces in between.

"What are they up to?" Deja asks.

Nikki squints her eyes. "I don't know."

"Looks like they're making some kind of train."

"No. They're too old to be making a pretend train."

"Then what are they doing?" Deja asks again.

Just then, Robert Turner glides up the street on his skateboard. He stops suddenly and stomps his board straight up. He watches the progress with the crates.

Nikki and Deja hear him say, "Whatcha doin'?"

"I'm gonna show Evan how to do a flat-ground Ollie," Darnell tells him.

That catches Nikki's and Deja's attention even more. What on earth is a flat-ground Ollie? They look at each other. Nikki reaches for her pad. Since she wants to be a news reporter when she grows up, she always keeps a pad of paper and a pen in a little pouch she wears around her neck. Deja watches her write:

> Darnell is going to show Evan
> how to do a Flat Ground Ollie.
> Evan looks scared.
> What's a Flat Ground Ollie?

Then they both turn their attention back across the street.

"Watch me," they hear Darnell say. He places one foot on his board, gives a shove with his other foot, then jumps on. When he is halfway down the block, he stops and does that tricky little kick that brings the board straight up, as if it is saluting him. "Now watch," he says again. "And get out of my way."

"He's bossy," Nikki whispers to Deja, though she knows the boys can't hear her. Deja doesn't say anything. She is busy waiting for the flat-ground Ollie.

Darnell starts slowly, then begins to build up speed, his sneakered foot moving in an easy rhythm. Just before he gets to the crates he's set up, he does something with his back foot that makes the skateboard tilt up in the front. Then it lifts up off the ground. He bends his knees and keeps his feet on the board. It sails over the boxes, with Darnell staying on easily, coming down with a loud thump on the other side. He rides it out, then stops abruptly, doing that little kick thing he seems to like so much.

"You try it!" Darnell calls out to Evan.

"I don't think Evan is going to be able to do that," Deja says to Nikki.

"I don't think so, either," Nikki agrees. She has a bad feeling.

Slowly, Evan rides his skateboard halfway down the block.

"He looks scared," Deja says.

Evan stops and turns around. He seems to be looking at the crates and measuring them in his mind.

"Come on!" Robert calls out. "What's takin' you so long?"

"This is not good," Deja says.

Then Evan starts up, gaining speed as he pumps away.

"Push on the back foot and bend your knees just before you get to the crates!" yells Darnell.

But instead of pushing on the back end of the board, instead of bending his knees and riding the board as it sails over the crates, Evan crashes into them, and his body crumples over.

Nikki holds her breath, her eyes as big as saucers. Deja holds her breath, too. Finally Deja says, "Oh, no . . ." Nikki is speechless. There is a long moment of stunned silence on both sides of the street.

Then Evan lets out a long wail. It starts low and begins to build, like a siren.

Darnell's front door flies open, and out stomps his mother in hair curlers. "What on earth! What on earth are you boys up to?" She rushes to Evan's side, looks down, then gently helps him up.

"Ow, ow, ow, ow," Evan wails. He is holding his arm funny and walking almost bent in half. "Ow, ow, ow!"

"Get in the house, Darnell!" his mother yells.

Suddenly, Darnell doesn't seem so big and bad. He looks scared, like he is going to get it. He meekly follows his mother and Evan into his house.

Nikki looks over at Deja and sees that her lips are drawn in, as if she is trying to keep from laughing.

"Are you going to laugh?" Nikki asks, shocked.

"Not at Evan—at Darnell." They watch Robert step on his skateboard and glide away. "Darnell looked so scared," Deja says. "And his mother looked so funny in those curlers."

Moments later, Darnell's mom, without the curlers, and Evan, with a tear-stained face, come out of the house. They get into her car. Nikki and Deja watch them slowly pull out of the driveway.

"Wonder where they're going?" Nikki says, more to herself than to Deja.

"To the hospital, what do you think?"

"Something's always happening on Fulton Street," Nikki says.

"Remember when Vianda's cat, Bianca, came back?" Deja asks.

"Oh, yeah." Nikki stops to remember the details. "She just came walking up the street after she'd been gone a real long time. And she had a split ear."

"And it's still split."

"And then, remember on Sunday, Mr. Robinson locked himself out of his house in his robe when he went to get the paper, and his wife was sound asleep and she wouldn't wake up and let him in?"

"That was so funny. He was pounding on the front door so loud, *I* woke up." Nikki and Deja laugh, remembering. Suddenly Nikki stops, and her eyes get big again. "We need a newspaper! A Fulton Street newspaper that tells all the stuff that happens on our street!"

Deja frowns. "We can't have a newspaper for just one street."

"Then we can have a newsletter. It can come out once a month. We can call it the *Fulton Street Newsy News Newsletter.*"

Deja looks off toward Mrs. Markham's rose-bushes. "What's newsy news?"

Nikki is ready with an answer. "News that's interesting. Not just saying someone planted a new rosebush. But like if their rosebush won a prize!" Nikki begins to feel excitement in her stomach. She can be the reporter. Deja can be the editor—whatever they do. This would help give her experience for when she grows up and becomes a real reporter. Nikki looks up the street.

Then she looks down the street. It is quiet and still, but she bets there are stories everywhere! Then she thinks of something—a little glitch. "Who's going to read our newsletter?"

"We'll get subscriptions," Deja says with confidence.

"How are we going to do that?"

"We'll type up a form on my auntie's computer, then we'll make copies, then we'll go door-to-door. And it's okay, because we know everybody on this street."

Nikki hesitates before asking the next question. "Should we charge money?"

"Of course," Deja says quickly.

"How much do you think, Deja?"

"A quarter," Deja says. "People don't think a quarter's all that much. They'll pay a quarter like that!" She snaps her fingers to emphasize her point.

Nikki considers this. The idea grows more and more appealing. How many houses are on Fulton Street? Just the part between Marin and Maynard? Maybe ten on each side. "Let's count the houses on both sides between Marin and Maynard Boulevard."

She jumps up and runs to the curb. She looks both ways and then runs across the street to the other side. "I'll count the houses on your side and you count the houses on mine," she calls to De

They meet back on Nikki's porch. There are exactly nine houses on each side of Fulton Street between Marin and Maynard Boulevard. They can't quite figure out how much money eighteen quarters are, so Nikki pulls out her notepad and kitty pen and begins to work out the problem. "We have to multiply," she says.

"I know that already," Deja says. She stares at the problem. "Ms. Shelby hasn't taught us how to do that kind of multiplication yet, though."

Ms. Shelby hasn't taught two-place multipliers yet, but Nikki's daddy had tried to explain it once. Nikki tries to solve the problem, but she can't remember how to do the steps. She decides it would be better to just go get a calculator. "I'm going to go get a calculator. I'll be back." She dis-

appears into the house and soon returns with her mom's calculator in her hand.

"Four dollars and fifty cents," Nikki says, once she's punched in the numbers. They both stare at the figure for a few seconds. "That's not very much. You try, Deja."

Deja takes her turn punching in the numbers. They see the same figure displayed.

"Maybe we can charge more. Like thirty cents," Nikki suggests.

"No, that's too complicated. Then people will have to find a nickel to go with the quarter, and if it's too hard, they'll hand you a dollar rather than go through the trouble, and you're all the time gonna be trying to make change."

Deja is right. *Deja always knows about these things,* Nikki thinks.

"We can have the newsletter come out twice a month rather than just once a month," Nikki offers.

Deja sighs. "Nikki, no street has that much news."

"Let's try it," Nikki says.

Deja shrugs, which is as good as saying okay.

They settle back on their elbows and look up and down the block. At that moment, Fulton Street looks as if it has no news at all. They are quiet for a bit, then Nikki says, "Ooh, ooh! We can write all about how I won the I Spy key chain from the grab bag."

Deja doesn't say anything.

"That would be good, wouldn't it, Deja?"

Deja sighs again, loudly, as if she is trying to show Nikki how weary she is of the topic. "Nikki, nobody wants to hear about you winning the I Spy key chain."

"It depends on how I write it. I can tell about how everyone wanted it, but nobody ever gets it and—"

"That's boring."

"It is not!" Nikki insists.

"You've already told that story a bunch of times." Deja looks away down the street as she says this.

"Well, it's just that it is the best prize in the grab bag, and no one's ever gotten it, and I'm the one who finally got it. That's all."

Deja doesn't say anything. She just looks up and rolls her eyes. Nikki catches this. "I think you're jealous," she says for the second time that day.

"No, I'm not. I like what *I* got."

That's not what she said before, Nikki thinks. "That mouse paper punch?"

"Yes. I always have papers I need to punch."

"Hmm." Now it's Nikki's turn to roll her eyes in disbelief. Deja had already told her how stupid she thought the hole puncher was. Before she can remind Deja of that, a car pulls up to Darnell's house and Evan's mother gets out and walks up to knock on the front door. Darnell's big sister answers. They speak for a few minutes, then Evan's mother makes an about-face and goes rushing back down the walkway to her car. She jumps in and speeds away.

"I guess she knows about Evan," Deja says.

3

The Fulton Street Newsy News Newsletter Is Born (Officially)

"Deja, I think we should include news about Carver Elementary, too," Nikki says as they walk to school the next morning.

Deja considers this for a moment. "Would people on our street want to hear about what's happening at our school?"

"Yeah, because it's a neighborhood school, and all their kids go there or used to go there, and my dad says that's one of the places our tax money goes to, so I think they'd be interested."

Nikki notices Deja stand up a little straighter at the mention of Nikki's dad. Probably because Deja's own dad hasn't been around for a long, long time. Deja has made it clear that she thinks Nikki's father is the smartest person in the world—just because he leaves the house every morning in a suit and tie and carries a briefcase. He works at some kind of company, and Deja has said that he probably does smart things all day long. "Okay," she agrees. "That would give us more stuff to write about."

Nikki smiles. She can't wait to get to school and start seeing things with a reporter's eye.

Just before recess, Ms. Shelby looks through the basket of class work to see who hasn't turned in their word lines. Only those who have done their work can go outside. "Ralph, I don't see your word lines," she says calmly.

Ralph jumps up out of his seat. "I turned it in!" he insists.

"Calm down. Let me look again." Now everyone turns toward Ms. Shelby with interest. A few look back at Ralph suspiciously.

"Ralph doesn't always do his work, Ms. Shelby," Rosario offers primly.

"But I turned it in this time!"

Ms. Shelby continues searching. Nikki sees a few children look up at the clock. They're probably thinking that this is cutting into their recess time. "Sorry, Ralph, I still don't see it. Would you like to look?"

Ralph marches up to the front of the class. To Nikki, he seems like a person who is telling the truth. He flips through the papers quickly. "Here it is!" He waves a paper in the air. "This is mine!"

Ms. Shelby studies the paper carefully. "This looks like your handwriting, I must say." She turns her gaze to Richard. "But it seems Richard has put his name on it."

She then dismisses the class row by row, keeping Richard behind to discuss the situation.

"He's going to have to write a letter to his mom about it," Ayanna says to Nikki and Deja as they hurry out the door. Ayanna has had plenty of practice writing letters home. The three of them walk to the handball court, but Nikki heads straight for the bench. She sits down and pulls out her kitty pen and notebook.

"Aren't you going to play?" Deja asks.

"I want to write something down first," Nikki says, looking off at nothing in particular and frowning slightly. Then she begins to write quickly.

"Whatever . . ." Deja says, and serves the ball.

For the entire school day, Nikki keeps her pad and kitty pen at the ready. She whips it out in the cafeteria when Carlos upsets Richard's carton of milk by accidentally bumping his tray. The milk spills onto Richard's lap, making an embarrassing wet spot down the front of his pants. He has to go to the office so the secretary can call home to have someone bring him another pair of pants.

In the afternoon, Nikki sees Carlton pass a note to Emilio. Emilio reads it and laughs to himself. He attempts to toss it to Ralph, but it lands short—right on Ayanna's desk. Ayanna reads it, and her eyes shift back and forth. She looks uncomfortable. She puts the folded paper in her desk.

As soon as they file out for P.E., Nikki sidles up to Ayanna and asks her what was in the note. "Just something about Yolanda being fat," Ayanna tells her. Nikki is disappointed, but then she thinks there might be something she can write about people being called fat and how it isn't nice.

After school, on the walk home, Nikki says, "I think I'm going to write about fat people and how it isn't nice to call them names or compare them to whales or barns."

"You can't do that," Deja says.

"Why not?"

"We aren't supposed to say 'fat' anymore. Remember when we got that talk?"

Nikki remembers, and she feels a little deflated. She really wants to mention that note in her newsletter. But Ms. Shelby's talks are very, very serious. Sometimes they are all-girl talks. Sometimes they are all boy. She'll hold the boys back from recess and have the girls go out, or

she'll hold the girls back. There is always a little ripple of excitement as everyone waits to see what she is going to say.

One time Ms. Shelby kept the whole class in to discuss the state in which they were leaving both restrooms. She looked almost hurt as she said, "Raise your hand if you would leave your own bathroom at home that way." A few eager beavers had their hands up before they digested the question. They lowered them sheepishly and looked around.

Ms. Shelby went on. Would they fill their own sinks at home with paper towels and then leave the water running? And what was so hard about getting their used paper towels into the big trash can in its convenient location right beside the sink? Would they walk away from their own toilets without bothering to flush? As Ms. Shelby talked, no one dared to look at anyone else. They'd been too worried that someone would think they were the guilty party.

Room Ten had had one of those special talks just the week before. Ms. Shelby let the boys out for recess and held the girls back. Then she'd turned to them with a really serious look on her face. Everyone waited. Finally, Ms. Shelby held up a folded piece of paper. She didn't say anything. She just scanned the group, lingering on one or two girls for an extra couple of seconds.

Then she opened the paper and held it up so it could be clearly seen. On the paper was a drawing of a whale, with a fountain of water shooting out of its blowhole. Someone had used the side of her pencil to shade it light gray. Then, across the body in dark pencil, were the words "Yolanda Meeker is as fat as a wale."

"I found this underneath a certain person's desk. I'm not sure that person is the one who drew this. It could have been anyone, actually. But I'm so glad Yolanda isn't here today. That way I can give you all fair warning without embarrassing her. What is one of our rules?" Every head had turned toward the class rules chart posted on the wall by the door.

"Treat everyone with respect," they said in unison. Beverly Cummings yawned a big, noisy yawn.

"It's rude to yawn out loud in front of a group, Beverly," Rosario said. Then she looked at Ms. Shelby expectantly. But Ms. Shelby just ignored her, and Beverly's yawn.

"If I see evidence of disrespect again, such as comparing people to whales or barns or whatever, I will have to make phone calls home."

Everyone seemed to hold their breath, then. Eyes shifted all around.

"All right," Ms. Shelby said. "You may go out to recess."

"It must have been under a girl's desk," Nikki had whispered to Deja as they'd walked out the door.

Now Nikki thinks that, in light of that talk, this latest disrespectful note is especially bad. Something needs to be done, and Nikki feels she is the one who should write about it. It is up to her to raise people's awareness. Ms. Shelby would want her to.

"I still think I'm going to write about people not calling other people fat," Nikki says to Deja as they reach Fulton Street.

"Not calling people fat is not a news story," Deja replies.

"I can write about how calling someone fat can hurt that fat person's feelings, and that some-one's feelings got hurt in our class . . . without mentioning Yolanda's name."

Deja doesn't answer. She is looking at Antonia's house down the street. Nikki looks, too. It seems particularly quiet. It is the only split-level house on Fulton Street—with a trampoline in the backyard and a tetherball built into the ground. Nikki and Deja have only seen the trampoline and tetherball once, when Antonia's family moved in. But they've heard all about them from Antonia.

Later, sitting at Auntie Dee's computer, which she said they could use if they were extra careful,

Deja composes this:

HOT OFF THE PRESSES!
THE FULTON STREET NEWSY NEWS NEWSLETTER
IS FINALLY HERE!
GET YOUR FIRST COPY! ONLY 25 CENTS!
YOU'LL GET IT EVERY OTHER WEEK!
IT WILL BE FULL OF NEWS ABOUT YOUR
NEIGHBORS ON FULTON STREET!

Name _____

Address _____

Phone number _____

Deja pulls the piece of paper out of the printer, and the two girls read it together.

"Well, I have a couple of questions," Nikki says.

"What?" Deja asks, sounding as if she is preparing to be testy. Nikki knows Deja can be a little sensitive, especially since she's composed the form all on her own.

"Don't you think that there are too many exclamation marks?"

"No, I don't."

Nikki goes on. "And why do we need their addresses? We know where everyone lives, and we're not mailing it. We're delivering it. And—"

"You said a *couple* of questions."

Nikki doesn't know how to ask the next question. Deja can be so bossy.

"What if . . ."

"What if, what?" Deja says, studying her order form with a look of satisfaction.

"What if no one wants our newsletter?"

"That's not the way to look at it, Nikki. You have to think everyone is going to want it. People always want to know about their neighbors."

Deja's words make Nikki feel a little uneasy. She doesn't think they are words her mother would approve of.

Deja jumps up and runs to the door of Auntie's office to peer into the living room.

"What's your auntie doing?" Nikki asks. She walks over to Deja and looks over her shoulder. Auntie Dee has her headphones on. She is listening to music and thumbing through a magazine. It is her winding-down time. "I need to unwind," she often says to Deja when she gets home from work, which is sometimes long after Deja gets home. Those afternoons, Deja stays at Nikki's until her aunt comes for her.

"She's unwinding."

"How come she has to unwind?"

"Because she's been working all day." Deja's aunt works for a small theater company, and according to her, she has to wear many hats. She has to raise funds, she has to see to publicity, and

she has to keep everyone happy. It's an exhausting job, Deja has told Nikki in the past.

Nikki thinks about this. "How do you unwind?"

"You do the opposite of working. Doesn't your dad have to unwind when he comes home from work?"

"I don't know. Maybe."

Deja goes back to the computer and checks the printer paper. "We have to print out eighteen of these. Auntie might not want me to use that much paper."

"Why don't you ask her?" Nikki says.

Deja looks over at Nikki for a long moment. "Nikki, if you don't want to hear no, you don't ask."

Nikki's eyes widen. "You're gonna get in trouble."

"Be quiet. No, I'm not."

They both turn to watch their order form being printed over and over and over again. When eighteen forms are stacked in the printer tray, Deja turns to Nikki. "You know what this means, don't you?"

"No, what?"

"The *Fulton Street Newsy News Newsletter* is officially born."

4

Editorial Decisions

Nikki and Deja have big plans for after school. As soon as they finish their homework and get a snack, they are going to go over all of their news stories and see which ones they want to put in the newsletter. Maybe they'll even decide on the stories before they do their homework.

"We're going to be famous," Deja says as they walk to school that morning.

"Famous?"

"For being the youngest people ever to have their own newspaper."

"Newsletter," Nikki says. "Kind of like our school newsletter that comes out every month."

Actually, Nikki doesn't think their newsletter, which will be full of real news, will be anything like the school newsletter. That newsletter comes out once a month and reports on boring things like field trips and which class had the highest attendance of parents at Back to School Night. Their newsletter is going to be way better.

The night before, on Auntie Dee's computer, Deja had pecked out a list of stories:

MRS. MARKHAM WINS BLUE RIBBON

EVAN BREAKS ARM BEING A DAREDEVIL

GLOBAL TIRE SLASHES PRICES

(Deja came up with that one by looking in their real newspaper and checking the lingo of real headlines.)

MR. ROBINSON LOCKED OUT

MISS IDA VISITS SHUT-INS

MR. BEACHAM'S BRAND-NEW GARDEN HOSE STOLEN! AND THE WINDER THING TOO!

(Deja heard Auntie mention that on the telephone to her friend Phoebe.)

BIANCA RETURNS

(She returned weeks before, but they needed some more news.)

Deja had convinced Nikki to let go of that article about fatness, even though Nikki still thought it was a good idea.

As soon as they enter the schoolyard, Nikki and Deja see Evan walk by with his arm in a cast.

"Wow, he really did break his arm," Nikki says.

"Toldja."

"You did not," Nikki replies.

"I knew he was going to break something."

In the classroom, Ms. Shelby is putting a new card in the lunch monitor envelope on the Job Squad chart. It looks like Ms. Shelby has received notice that Valerie is going to be absent, and Antonia is getting the coveted lunch monitor job in her place. Everyone wants to be lunch monitor. It is a special job Ms. Shelby has created because she has grown tired of the noise level in the cafeteria. The lunch monitor is in charge of a small spiral notebook that has the words LUNCH MONITOR on it. She or he gets to report on any bad manners at the lunch table, which include mixing food not to be mixed (pudding and milk, for example); throwing away whole, untouched apples or cartons of milk; grabbing at another person's food or even asking for it; throwing food; and shouting in any way, shape, or form.

The best part of being lunch monitor is making the after-lunch report. While the monitor consults the spiral notebook, everyone looks at him or her suspiciously. As soon as anyone's name and offense is recounted, that person is already jumping up to protest. Especially the boys. Ms. Shelby doesn't accept protests if there are witnesses to the offenses. She just walks over to the behavior chart next to the whiteboard and switches the green behavior card to orange—the warning color.

At lunch Antonia takes her special seat at the end of the long cafeteria table. She keeps a sharp eye on her classmates while she eats. Gerald blows bubbles in his milk. Quietly, Antonia opens her notebook and jots that down. Gerald pays no attention. Leslie laughs, with chewed-up food clearly visible. Again, out comes the notebook, more notations entered.

Nikki watches this uneasily. She doesn't like the way Antonia acts when she is lunch monitor. It's as if all she wants to do is catch someone doing something wrong. Nikki takes a sip of milk. Maybe she should warn Leslie, who seems to be taking great pleasure in grossing everyone out. Nikki looks down at the untouched apple on her tray. She doesn't want it, but she can't throw it away—not when children are starving in parts of the world, as Ms. Shelby always reminds them.

Nikki takes a big bite of apple. Then Arthur catches her attention. He is blowing through his straw to make the straw paper roll out, then back in, like one of those party favor toys. That doesn't escape Antonia's notebook, either. Out it comes for another entry.

In the yard after lunch, most of the girls in Ms.

Shelby's class get caught up in a game of waterfall with the two long ropes. Before they know it, the freeze bell is ringing and it is time to line up.

The first thing everyone has to do upon entering the classroom is pull out their Sustained Silent Reading books and begin reading for ten minutes. This is to be done without talking. Ralph usually just stares at the pages, Nikki notices, never turning them. Just staring at them with his chin on the desk. Nikki is tempted to point this out to Ms. Shelby, but she would probably remind Nikki that she has enough to do taking care of herself.

Actually, sometimes Nikki just stares at the pages as well, whenever she feels like thinking more than reading. On this day she wants to think of how Antonia acts whenever she is lunch monitor. She doesn't even give a warning. It is almost as if she is happy to catch people breaking the rules.

Nikki looks over at Deja now. She is reading a book about howler monkeys. On the cover is a longhaired monkey swinging from a tree, its mouth open just like a big *O*. Deja is mouthing the words, even though Ms. Shelby has told them to try to read without doing that.

Soon, Sustained Silent Reading time is finished. They get to put their books away, to the relief of some but the dismay of others. It is time for Antonia to give her report. It is time for some behavior cards to go from green to orange.

"Antonia, do you have a report to make?" Ms. Shelby asks.

Antonia stands up and takes the small spiral notebook out of her pencil box. She flips it to the right page. She looks around. She begins. "Leslie was laughing with her mouth open with chewed-up food in it so that we could all see it."

Leslie frowns. Ms. Shelby looks as if she is trying to keep from smiling.

"Remember what I said, class. Only make a note of the behaviors we talked about: rough-housing, playing with food, throwing away food that's been untouched, shouting . . ."

Nikki notices that the whole time Ms. Shelby is saying this, Antonia is looking down, with her mouth pursed. Nikki knows that look. Antonia is not pleased. Nikki can guess what she is thinking. People who show their chewed-up food should not be excused.

Antonia goes on: Arthur was shooting the paper off his straw. Gerald blew bubbles in his chocolate milk, then sucked some up and shot it across the table at Jose. She pauses then. "That's it," she says, sounding almost disappointed. She is about to sit down when she jumps back up again. "Oh, and Deja didn't eat all of her apple. She threw away most of it."

Deja opens her mouth to protest, but Ms. Shelby silences her with a look.

"I noticed it on her tray at the last minute, so I didn't get a chance to put it in the notebook, Ms. Shelby."

Nikki feels like protesting as well. She remembers Deja's apple. It was mostly eaten.

Ms. Shelby sighs and puts Arthur's and Gerald's orange cards in front of their green cards. "I'm hoping I can replace these with green by day's end," she says. Antonia puts away the lunch monitor notebook and sits down.

"As for you, Deja," Ms. Shelby continues, "you have to try to eat what's put on your tray—at least most of it. Not just a couple of bites. I'm giving you a warning this time." Deja looks like it is all she can do to keep her mouth shut.

Later, on the way home from school, Deja says, "That dumb Antonia. What's her problem? I didn't think she still had it in for me. After all, I did invite her to my birthday party out of the goodness of my heart."

"Maybe she didn't see it that way," Nikki says. "Maybe she thought your auntie made you invite her."

"Oh, whatever," Deja says, then changes the subject. "Don't forget. We're getting subscriptions today."

"Uh-huh," Nikki says.

Deja looks over at Nikki with a questioning look on her face, as if checking to see if Nikki is in full agreement.

Nikki sighs. "I don't think it's right that Antonia is trying to get so many kids in trouble. I don't think that's helpful," she says. "I think I'm going to write about how when people get to be a monitor, it shouldn't be just to get other kids in trouble. I'm going to add it to this week's newsletter."

"Yeah. She can't be trying to get people in trouble all the time, just for fun. That's not right," Deja agrees.

They reach Deja's house. Deja sees Auntie's car in the driveway. She must have gotten out of work early. "Let's hurry up and get permission to get subscriptions to our newsletter," Deja says.

"Deja, we need to write the newsletter first."

"We can write it after we get subscriptions."

"But then people will be paying for nothing," Nikki says.

"No, because it's not gonna take us long to write our newsletter. Probably just a couple of hours."

"Deja, it's going take longer than that. Let's get the subscriptions afterward."

Deja seems to think about this. "Okay," she says.

Nikki is right. It takes more time to write the newsletter than Deja said it would, even though each article is not more than a paragraph. They both write, then Nikki edits and revises a little bit, just like Ms. Shelby has taught them. Deja types because she can hunt and peck faster.

Nikki looks up from scanning Deja's latest paragraph and says in an exasperated voice, "Deja, why can't you write neater? I can't read what you've written here."

Deja stops her hunting and pecking and snatches the handwritten page out of Nikki's hand. She squints at the paper. It seems she can't read it herself. "Oh," she says finally. "It says, 'People who are bad monitors shouldn't be monitors at all. They . . .'" Deja stops and peers at the

paper. After a long moment, she says, "Well, you write it, then. It's about how dumb Antonia is, trying to get me in trouble."

Nikki sighs deeply. This is going to take way longer than she thought.

When they finish, it doesn't exactly look like a newsletter. It is plain, and it doesn't have columns. Each paragraph is in a different-colored type. Deja has changed the headlines to sound more like news. And she's added a bunch of exclamation marks:

MRS. MARKHAM'S ROSES VIEWED BY THOUSANDS!

SERIOUS ACCIDENT ON FULTON STREET!

BAD MONITORS AT CARVER ELEMENTARY!

PRICES SLASHED AT GLOBAL TIRE!

MR. ROBINSON LOCKED OUT OF HIS OWN HOUSE!

MISS IDA VISITS SHUT-INS!

VIANDA'S CAT FINALLY COMES HOME!

"I didn't put in these exclamation marks," Nikki says. "Like, 'Miss Ida Visits Shut-ins!' It's stupid to top that off with an exclamation mark."

"I just want people to be excited."

"You can't force people to be excited, Deja."

Deja looks off to the side, but says nothing. Their newsy newsletter is only one page—

front and back. And it only covers both sides of the page because they've used a big font. Now all they have to do is print one side, then stick the paper back into the printer face-up and print the other side. Because they use a different color for each article, the last few newsletters are a bit faded. The color ink is running low.

"We're ready to sell!" Deja exclaims. She runs to the bottom of the stairs and yells up to where Auntie Dee is talking on the telephone in her bedroom. "Auntie Dee, can me and Nikki go for a walk?"

Auntie Dee comes to the top of the stairs and looks down. She squints suspiciously. "A walk?"

"Just for twenty minutes, and we'll stay on this street. It's a Friday . . ." Deja adds, a little whine to her voice.

"Twenty minutes," Auntie Dee says. "And I'd better be able to look out the window and see you."

"Okay." Deja turns to Nikki. "Come on, let's go."

5

Selling Newsy News

"I'll take this side, and you take across the street," Deja says.

"Wait a minute. I'm not getting it," Nikki says, frowning.

"What is it now, Nikki?"

"We're selling the newsletter and getting subscriptions at the same time?"

"Yeah," Deja says. "Once they see the newsletter, they're gonna want a subscription."

"But they're going to have to fill out stuff and then get the money. That's going to take more than twenty minutes. Why don't we just sell the paper without all that subscription stuff?"

"But I like our subscription form, and anyway, what are we going to do with all those forms?

Nikki thinks about this. "The recycle bin?"

"Wait a minute, Nikki. We need those forms. They're going to be for the people who aren't home. We're going to put them in their mail-boxes."

"Are they going to mail them to us? They can just walk them over."

"Nikki, why are you making things so compli-cated? We need to get started. We're wasting time."

There is no answer at the first house Nikki goes to. For some reason she is glad. She has nine sub-scription forms and nine newsletters. She slides a subscription form into the mail slot. One house down and eight to go. Actually, she'd rather slip a subscription form into everyone's box. She is a little nervous at the thought of talking to people about the newsletter.

Nikki looks across the street. Deja is already talking to Mrs. Cheevers. She and her husband are retirees. Mrs. Cheevers is fishing around in a little change purse and plucking out a quarter. Nikki watches Deja do an about-face and strut down the Cheeverses' walkway, head held high. She looks confident.

Slowly, Nikki approaches the front door of the next house. She reaches up and rings the doorbell. She waits, listening. She looks at the pots of geraniums on either side of the door. It is

Vianda's house. It looks different and feels different this close up. She can hear footsteps. Her heart sinks. Then the door is opening.

"Hey, girl, whatcha want?" Vianda says. She has on a purple sweat suit, and she looks as if she is in the middle of cornrowing her hair. Half is hanging loose, and half is tightly braided.

Nikki, suddenly nervous, almost forgets what it is that she wants. But Vianda's warm smile puts her at ease.

"I've got this newsletter that me and Deja made, and we're selling it for a quarter. If you want to buy it," Nikki adds.

"Newsletter . . . hmm," Vianda says. "Let me see it."

Nikki hands it over and holds her breath.

Vianda scans it, then looks up at Nikki and winks. She turns it over, reads a little bit, then bursts out laughing. "This is funny," she says. "I remember that, too—Mr. Robinson getting locked out of his house last Sunday morning. He woke me up." She keeps reading, and Nikki begins to grow worried. If Vianda reads the whole thing just standing there, why would she need to buy it? An image of people lingering at the newsstand, reading whatever they want so they won't have to pay for stuff, flashes in her mind. Maybe Vianda is going to read the newsletter front to back and then not pay for it.

"This is some funny stuff," Vianda says. "And Bianca's in it. I'll buy it." She pulls a small zippered purse from the pocket of her sweat suit top. "Here's a quarter." She drops a quarter into Nikki's hand. "Wait, here's another one for any future issue." She drops another quarter into Nikki's hand. Nikki slips them into her pocket, feeling relieved.

The next house is Darnell's. Nikki feels funny approaching the house of someone from Carver Elementary. She climbs the steps and rings the doorbell. She looks around. There is Darnell's skateboard at the far end of the porch, looking abandoned. She hasn't seen him on his skateboard, in fact, since the accident. His skateboard looks huge, somehow. While she is thinking about this, the door opens. She is dismayed to see that it is Darnell.

"What do you want?" he asks rudely.

"Me and Deja are selling this newsletter. It's all about our block. And a few things about Carver," she adds.

He extends his hand, but doesn't step out. "Let me see it."

Nikki doesn't want to just let him see it. In fact, she'd rather let his mom or dad see it. It feels like Darnell will be a waste of time. She hands over a copy and waits while he looks it over, scowling the whole time.

"Uh-uh!" he says suddenly. "This ain't right. You got this wrong." He'd gotten to the part about Evan's accident. "I wasn't havin' him do somethin' dangerous. The flat-ground Ollie is not dangerous! He just didn't do it like I told him. If he'd done it right, there wouldn't have been a problem."

Nikki stands there, looking down. She feels it is best not to say anything.

"You shouldn't put something in a newsletter that's not right."

"Well, I kind of think it was dangerous for Evan," she says quietly.

"Not if he'd done like I told him."

"Do you think your parents would like a subscription to our newsletter? It's going to come out once every two weeks."

"This looks stupid," he says as he returns the newsletter to her with a sneer.

"Can you give them this subscription form?"

"No, I cannot," he says, and shuts the door.

She stands in front of the closed door for a few seconds, then sticks a subscription form in the mailbox mounted on the porch post and skips down the steps. She is happy to be walking away from Darnell's house rather than toward it.

The next house is Auntie Dee's friend Phoebe's. Nikki rings the doorbell. Phoebe opens the door. "Hi, honey," she says warmly. "What can I do for you?" There is a heavenly aroma drifting out of her kitchen. Brownies. Nikki is momentarily caught off-guard, thinking of brownies.

"We're selling this newsletter," she says when she finally finds her voice.

"Newsletter?" Phoebe takes it out of her hand and studies it for a bit. "Jo Markham's flowers are featured in some kind of magazine?"

Again, Nikki is caught off-guard. She's never thought of Mrs. Markham as having a first name. And not such a modern-sounding and short one as Jo.

"How much you want for this newsletter?" Phoebe asks with smiling eyes.

"It costs a quarter," Nikki says.

"That's a bargain. Be right back." She turns and starts for the kitchen. Not only does she come back with a quarter, she is holding a warm brownie on a green napkin.

"Here, sweetie pie," she says, handing Nikki the quarter. After Nikki deposits the quarter in her jeans pocket, Phoebe puts the delicious-smelling brownie in her hand.

"Thank you," Nikki says.

"My pleasure."

That's the way it goes for the rest of the block. A few people aren't home, so she just sticks subscription forms in their mailboxes. But the ones who are home readily buy the newsletter and promise to buy the next issue as well. Nikki feels a real sense of accomplishment when she heads back to her porch, where she is to meet Deja. She has her brownie, and it is still kind of warm. She is waiting for Deja to return before taking the first bite. It is just something she is compelled to do. Nikki is pretty sure Deja hasn't gotten a brownie on her side of the street. This way she can nibble at it in front of Deja and make her wish she had one.

"Where did you get that?" Deja asks as soon as she returns and sees the brownie on its green napkin, perched on Nikki's bent knees.

"Auntie Dee's friend Phoebe."

"Let me have some."

Nikki twists her mouth to the side, thinking. "Okay, I'll give you a little bite, and I mean a little one." Nikki holds it out, but as Deja bends forward, it seems as if she is positioning herself to take a big bite. Nikki snatches it away just in time. "I said a little bite."

"I was going to take a little bite," Deja says.

"It looked like you were going to take a big bite."

"I was going to take a little bite. Now let me have some."

"I'm going to break it off," Nikki says, breaking

off a piece before Deja can protest. She holds it out to Deja, and Deja snatches it out of Nikki's hand, sucking her tongue at the same time.

"You didn't even say thank you," Nikki complains.

"*Thank* you," Deja says, then pops it into her mouth.

Deja has collected six quarters. She only left one subscription form, because she skipped over their own houses. Nikki has collected five quarters—six, if she counts the extra one Vianda's given her. She left four subscription forms. They plan to divide the money later, after more people pay for subscriptions and it's all collected. They go into their houses to do their homework.

6

Trampolines and Tetherballs Built into the Ground

The problem with putting out a newsy news newsletter every other week is that the days seem to race by. Suddenly it is Wednesday, and the second newsy news newsletter is due on Friday.

On the way to school Nikki says, "Deja, we need news for Friday's newsletter."

"We'll get news. I'm not worried."

And she doesn't seem to be. When Nikki looks over at Deja, she has a smooth, calm look on her face.

In the classroom, once morning journals are open on every desk and everyone has been writing awhile, Ms. Shelby scans the seats for absences and says, "Antonia's out again." She says this under her breath, as if she is just making an observation to herself.

Deja looks up, then glances over at Antonia's empty seat. Nikki's eyes meet hers. They both look at Antonia's vacant desk.

Antonia was absent on Monday, Tuesday, and now Wednesday as well. Maybe she has the flu or something. Maybe she has the chickenpox. Nikki thinks of Antonia with chickenpox. Nikki had it when she was four. It was awful. Chickenpox on the bottom of her feet, chickenpox in her ears. She imagines Antonia covered with chickenpox all over. Where *is* Antonia? Why hasn't she been at school all week?

Deja poses this question as she and Nikki walk home that afternoon.

"It's kind of mysterious," Nikki says. "Plus, hasn't her house been looking strange?"

"Strange how?" asks Deja.

"Like nobody's there."

As they reach their block, they slow to get a good look at Antonia's house. It does seem as if no one is home. The drapes are drawn, and there is a quietness that the other houses on the street don't have.

"Where is everybody?" Nikki asks.

No cars in the driveway. "They've gone on vacation," says Deja.

"They wouldn't go on vacation in the middle of the school year," Nikki says.

Deja seems to be thinking of something.

She stops. She stands staring at Antonia's house.

"What are you doing?" Nikki asks.

"I want to see her trampoline."

"How are you going to do that?"

Deja doesn't answer. She crosses the street and starts toward the driveway. Nikki looks both ways, then follows, but stays on the sidewalk looking after her. "What are you doing, Deja?"

"I just want to take a peek at that trampoline."

"What if someone sees you?"

Again, Deja doesn't answer. She just keeps on walking up the driveway. Nikki looks around. She follows. "Deja . . . come back."

On the side of the house, there is a tall gate with a latch in the middle that can be flipped up to allow the gate to open. Deja releases the latch and steps through the gate. Nikki is close behind. They both look back over their shoulders, up at a window that might be the kitchen window. The curtain is drawn. They look above that window to another window at the back of the split part of Antonia's split-level house. There is a curtain drawn there as well.

"Deja . . ." Nikki says in a loud whisper.

Deja whips her head around and frowns, poking her lips out. "Shhh!"

Her face looks kind of like a monster, Nikki thinks. She is a little scared, but she follows anyway.

Antonia's house has a long, covered porch in

the back. There are hanging pots of geraniums. *This is probably where they all sit and have their family cookouts in the summer,* Nikki thinks as she notes the patio table and chairs.

"Come on, Deja. Come on, let's go," Nikki says.

"Wait!" Deja hisses. She is staring at the trampoline. Nikki knows that Deja is thinking about all the times they've had to hear about that trampoline and that stupid tetherball built into the ground. Deja starts toward it.

"What are you doing?" Nikki says with alarm as she watches Deja give the tetherball a hard whack. "Let's go, let's go, let's go!"

"Okay, okay. Nobody's home anyway." Deja looks at the trampoline again.

Nikki catches that look. "No, Deja."

Deja rolls her eyes and sighs. "Okay. Come on." She turns and starts toward the gate. But just then they hear a car pulling into the driveway. They stop in their tracks. Eyes wide, they stare at each other. Nikki brings her hand to her mouth, and they both look at the gate. It is unlatched and slightly ajar.

The girls look around. The backyard has a tall cinderblock wall surrounding it. There is no way they can climb over it. "We're going to get in big trouble," Nikki says, sounding as if she is about to cry.

"No, we're not," Deja says, spying the gardening shed at the back of the yard.

"This is trespassing," Nikki whines. "This is against the law."

They hear a car door slam. Again they look at each other. Deja grabs Nikki by the hand. "We're not going to get in trouble," she repeats, leading Nikki toward the gardening shed.

It is dark in there and smells like wet dirt. It is crowded with bags of grass seed and bags of manure. There are clay pots of all kinds and tools hanging on hooks on the walls. In the middle there is a small wooden worktable.

"We're staying here for a while," Deja says.

"My mom's going to be real mad." Nikki begins to whimper. "She's going to wonder how come I'm not home already."

Deja is busy rubbing the inside pane of the shed's small window with the sleeve of her hoodie. She peers out. "As soon as whoever that is goes in the house, we're gonna leave."

"They might see us!"

"Shh, be quiet!" Deja orders. Someone is approaching the gate. It is Antonia's father. Deja quickly lowers her head, then slowly raises up so she can just see out. Nikki looks, too. They can see the top of Antonia's father's head. He seems to be standing on the other side of the gate, staring at it. Nikki feels her heart beating faster. They

are going to be in so much trouble. They hear the gate being latched and then hear Antonia's father walking away. Soon the front door of the house slams shut.

"Come on," Deja says, grabbing Nikki's arm. They run on tiptoes to the gate, all the time keeping their eyes on the windows with the drawn curtains. Carefully, and as quietly as possible, Deja pushes the latch up. The gate creaks a little as she eases it open just a bit.

Then Antonia's father comes out of the house again, and they freeze. They wait just inside the gate as he puts a small suitcase into the car trunk and slams it shut. As soon as he goes back into the house, they slip through the gate and quickly make their way down the driveway.

Once on the sidewalk, Nikki and Deja let out the big breaths they'd been holding. Then they begin to run. They run across the street all the way to Nikki's front porch. Auntie isn't going to be home until late, so Deja has to stay at Nikki's.

As soon as they step through Nikki's front door, her mom appears in the kitchen doorway. "Where were you?" she asks. "You know to come straight home."

Nikki stands there with her lips pressed together. Deja is watching her, as if waiting to see what she will say. Nikki always wants to tell the truth, but she knows the truth will get back to Deja's Auntie Dee, and then Deja might get in trouble. She'd like to say nothing, but her mother is waiting.

"We went to Antonia's house," Nikki says.

Her mother frowns, looking perplexed. "The little girl who lives across the street?"

Nikki nods. It is the truth. They had gone to Antonia's house. Just not to play with Antonia.

Deja looks back and forth from Nikki to Nikki's mom and back to Nikki again, as if she is trying to judge how this is going over.

"I thought you didn't like her," Nikki's mom says.

"We like her okay," Nikki says.

Not . . . Deja's expression seems to say.

"Well, next time, get permission before you go someplace after school. I was just about to worry."

"Okay," Nikki says, looking at Deja. "Can we get a snack?"

"Yes, but don't spoil your dinner," Nikki's mom replies.

Later, as they sit at the kitchen table with graham crackers and peanut butter, Nikki says, "It wasn't really a lie, what I said."

"Uh-huh, yes it was, Nikki," Deja says. "You know we're not friends with Antonia."

"Why aren't we friends with her?" Nikki asks, frowning a little.

"Because she's stuck-up, that's why." Deja squints at Nikki, as if she is trying to see if Nikki has changed her mind about Antonia.

"Maybe she isn't all that stuck-up," Nikki says.

Deja presses her lips together.

"I wonder where she is," Nikki muses. She licks some peanut butter off her graham cracker.

Deja shrugs. "Who knows? Who cares?"

7

Slow News—No News

Later, after their homework is done and they have gotten permission to go outside, they walk up and down Fulton Street. They need stories by Friday. They pass Miss Ida's, where Deja had stayed once when Auntie Dee had to go out of town. Nikki taps her pad with her pen. It feels as if her pen is itching to write something, but there is nothing to write.

"We already wrote about Miss Ida and the shut-ins."

"Yeah," says Deja. "We can't do that again."

They pass Mr. Robinson's house. Nothing is happening there. "It would be great if he could lock himself out of his house again, in his robe," Nikki says.

"That's not going to happen."

Nothing's shaking at Darnell's house, either.

He's still not back on his skateboard. He's probably still banned from it.

They get to the end of the street, cross over, and start down the other side. What a dull afternoon. Not one person is even out watering the lawn.

"Maybe we should walk down Maynard Boulevard," Deja suggests.

"We can't do that without permission," Nikki says.

"One of the stores could be having a sale."

Just then they see a Bugs Away van pulling out of the Denvers' driveway. On the side of the vehicle there is a picture of an enormous water bug turned onto its back, with all its spindly legs waving in the air.

"Yuck," Deja says. "They must be having bug problems."

"Maybe roaches," says Nikki, wrinkling her nose in distaste.

Deja considers this silently. They walk on. They get to the end of the block and turn back toward their own houses.

In school the next day there is no Antonia for the fourth day in a row. Ms. Shelby says something under her breath again as she scans the classroom and makes her notations. She still seems to be puzzled by Antonia's absence. Nikki thinks she'll probably get in touch with Antonia's mother

to find out why. No news forthcoming there.

The whole morning is blah. Nothing eventful happens. And they even serve blah three-bean salad in the cafeteria. Nikki stares down at it with a sense of dread. She can't toss it, because Rosario is sitting at the end of the cafeteria table with the lunch monitor notebook. Plus, Nikki would only think of the starving children in the world and feel guilty. She manages to get three bites down with the help of gulps of milk and chicken nuggets. Deja taught her this trick after she had to eat yucky turnips at Miss Ida's.

The afternoon is equally blah. Nikki is in Group Three in math and gets to do all kinds of enriched stuff. The kids in Group Three can work independently after Ms. Shelby explains things. Deja is in Group Two. Nikki knows that they are both glad they aren't in the group that always has to be brought to the kidney-shaped table for extra help.

It is during math that Ayanna Ford suddenly yells out that her book-order money is missing from her backpack.

Ms. Shelby looks up from the group she is helping at the special table. "Are you sure, Ayanna?" She gets up to help Ayanna search for it.

"It was in the little zipper part! I put it in there this morning when I was putting in my home-work folder!" She still seems to find it necessary to shout.

"Calm down, Ayanna." Ms. Shelby takes Ayanna's backpack out of her hand and begins to unpack it on Ayanna's desk. Everything is in that backpack. Balled papers, old work pages, spelling tests that should have been put in her assessment binder along with all the other tests Ms. Shelby has passed back. A bunch of story booklets that are supposed to be taken home every week for reading practice, markers and colored pencils, half of an eraser . . .

"Honestly, Ayanna," Ms. Shelby says. "This is a mess." But Ayanna is right. There is no white envelope with her book-order money. "Are you sure you put it in here?"

"I'm sure." Ayanna's eyes begin to fill with tears.

"Class," Ms. Shelby says, "does anyone know where Ayanna's money can be?"

Nikki wonders about Ms. Shelby's question. What good is it? The few other times someone's money went missing, Ms. Shelby always started off with phrases that gave everyone the benefit of the doubt. Nikki thought this was not the right approach, because no one was going to just step forward and admit to taking it. If Nikki were Ms. Shelby, she'd do a search right then. She'd have everybody turn their pockets inside out and then put on their jackets and turn those pockets inside out. Then she'd have everyone empty their backpacks and their desks and take their shoes off. Especially Calvin Vickers. Things are always winding up in his desk. Other kids' markers, their erasers, some small toy that someone brought to class, against school rules. . . . In fact, Nikki has the notion to raise her hand and suggest that Ms. Shelby thoroughly check Calvin Vickers, but something makes her think better of it.

When Ms. Shelby doesn't get a response, she sighs. "Okay, everyone, take everything out of your desks. I'll check the backpacks." Nikki looks at the long row of backpacks hanging on their hooks on the wall above the cubbies. *This is more like it,* she thinks smugly. She looks over at Calvin Vickers. He is crashing crayons together, looking pleased to have this little break from work. She almost smiles, thinking of him getting his comeuppance.

However, Calvin Vickers's backpack contains only Calvin Vickers's junk, including a moldy chicken sandwich.

"What is this, Calvin?" Ms. Shelby says when she plucks it out with two fingers. "Calvin Vickers—throw this away!"

He takes it out of her hand as if there is nothing at all wrong with having a moldy chicken sandwich in your backpack. Nikki imagines him thinking, *What's the big deal?*

The money isn't in any of the backpacks. It

isn't in any of the desks. The only good thing about not finding the money is that everyone's desk gets a good cleaning out.

Deja and Nikki discuss the missing money on their way home. Deja is certain Calvin Vickers is the culprit. Nikki couldn't agree more.

"This is what I think," says Deja. "He could've taken the money out during recess. Maybe he pretended to have to go back into the classroom for his snack or something. And maybe Ms. Shelby was in the teachers' lounge having her tea. Plus, people have been bringing in book-order money all week, but they know Ms. Shelby won't be turning it in until Friday. And maybe Ayanna told people that she had book money in her backpack. He could have taken it then."

Nikki thinks about this with squinting eyes. Suddenly, she has doubts. "I don't know, Deja. Where'd he put it? Ms. Shelby searched everything."

"She didn't search everyone's shoes."

"True," Nikki says.

"He could have put the money in his shoe, thinking Ms. Shelby might check pockets, and he could have thrown away the envelope in one of the trash cans in the yard."

"I don't know."

"I betcha it was Calvin Vickers," Deja says, staring straight ahead, as if she can just envision it.

8

Antonia Mystery "Solved"

Once again, Fulton Street looks lifeless. Nikki and Deja sit on Deja's porch. Deja's favorite stuffed animal, Bear, sits collecting dust on the porch swing behind them. Up and down the street they look. Nothing, *nada*.

"What are we going to do, Deja?" Nikki asks. "We have to get the newsletter done by tomorrow afternoon."

"I don't know." Deja taps her forehead, as if that will give her an idea or two. "Let's see if we can go to the store."

Deja goes into her house to get permission from Auntie Dee, and Nikki runs next door to her own house to ask her mother.

"We have to walk directly there and directly back," Nikki says when she returns.

"Yeah, that's what Auntie Dee said, too."

They start toward Maynard and Mr. Delvecchio's market. Just as they are passing Antonia's house, the door opens and out comes Antonia's mother, her arms loaded with stuffed animals. She puts them in the trunk of her car, slams it closed, and gets in the driver's seat. She starts up the car and drives off, not looking at them once.

"I know why Antonia hasn't been at school," Deja says excitedly.

"How do you know?"

"Don't you get it?" Deja asks. "Didn't you see what she just did?"

"She put some stuffed animals in her trunk and drove away."

"Right. She and Antonia have moved. She probably has to get those so Antonia will feel at home at their new place. Where she and Antonia live now."

Nikki thinks about this.

Deja goes on. "And now only Antonia's father lives there. That's why Antonia hasn't been at school. She's moved away."

This kind of makes sense to Nikki, but there is just one question. "Why do they live somewhere else?"

"Because they had a big fight and Antonia's mother is mad and Antonia is on her mother's side."

"Antonia's parents had a big fight?" This

makes Nikki feel uneasy. She immediately thinks of her own parents.

"A really big fight," Deja says with certainty.

They walk back home in silence—a serious silence—but with a bag of hot chips from Mr. D's market between them.

"We'll see if she comes to school tomorrow," Deja says.

The next morning, they take their seats and watch the door of their classroom as each straggler walks in. Ralph is tardy as usual and is looking sheepish. He always ducks his head as he enters late. Then there is Ayanna coming in with a tardy slip extended toward Ms. Shelby. She's usually not late. "Where's your tardy slip, Ralph?" Ms. Shelby asks. He makes a U-turn back out the door. After a few moments, Nikki and Deja look at each other. No Antonia. This is news.

As soon as the class is let out at recess, they make a beeline for the outdoor lunch benches. Those with snacks are confined to that area during recess.

"Let's add Antonia to our list," Deja says. "Take out your pad."

"What list?" Nikki asks, but takes out her pad anyway.

"For our newsletter. We're going to put Antonia in it."

As soon as they get home, Nikki makes an appearance at her house and then runs over to Deja's. They have work to do. First, they start with their headlines.

SNEAKY THIEF IN ROOM TEN!

BUG PROBLEM AT THE DENVERS'

NEW SCHOOL FOR ANTONIA

MISS IDA VISITS NIECE
(Deja heard this from Auntie Dee.)

STILL NO SKATEBOARDING FOR DARNELL

OVERPRICED FOOD AT SIMPLY
DELICIOUS HEALTH FOOD STORE
(Again, overheard from Auntie Dee.)

GREASY FOOD AT PUERTO NUEVO
(Yet another item Deja overheard when Auntie Dee was on the phone with her friend Phoebe.)

Deja looks over her headlines with a smile. She was the one who came up with them. Nikki is glad that Deja remembered a couple of choice items from Auntie Dee's telephone conversations with Phoebe to fill up the last part of the second page.

They work until almost dinnertime, then print out a copy. Nikki looks it over and finds the typos and misspellings. Once Deja makes the corrections, she prints out the rest of the copies in color. Auntie had replaced the color ink after puzzling over how fast it had been used up.

"Auntie Dee," Deja says from the kitchen doorway. Auntie is chopping zucchini for a vegetable casserole.

"What, honeybunch?"

"Can we go out and deliver our newsletter? Just on this block," Deja adds quickly.

"Newsletter?" Auntie asks.

"Me and Nikki made a newsletter for our block. Can we go out and deliver it? Just on this block?"

"I guess so," Auntie says slowly, as if she isn't all the way sure, but she doesn't know why.

Nikki and Deja dash out before she can change her mind.

"We did it!" Deja says when they reach the walkway. She gives Nikki half of the newsletters. "I'm taking that side this time," Deja announces. Nikki suspects that Deja wants a chance at one of Phoebe's freshly baked brownies.

It doesn't take long. People know about the newsletter already. Those who weren't home the week before can finally make sense of the strange subscription form they'd found in their mailboxes. They are happy to buy the latest issue for a quarter.

Deja and Nikki meet up on Nikki's porch in record time. "We did it," they can't help saying again—at the same time. They slap palms.

9

Big Problems at the Fulton Street Newsy News Newsletter

On Monday, as soon as they finish writing about their weekends in their morning journals, Ms. Shelby has an announcement to make.

"I feel so negligent," Ms. Shelby says. "I just learned that your classmate Antonia had an appendicitis attack and had to have an operation. She's home now and doing okay, but we really should make get-well cards for her." She turns to the kidney table to begin moving things out of the way so she can call up the slow readers.

"Oh yes, one more thing," she says over her shoulder. "I'm happy to say that Mrs. Broadie, in the cafeteria, found Ayanna's envelope of book money under a lunch table on Friday." She looks over at Ayanna. "You can pick it up in the office at recess, Ayanna." Ayanna grins happily.

Deja closes her mouth, which had been hanging open, and looks at Nikki. Nikki looks at her at the same time. She thinks of the paragraph they put in the newsletter about Antonia.

Antonia Barkley has moved to a new neighborhood and a new school, leaving behind her trampoline and tetherball built into the ground that she's told us about so many times. She's moved with her mother. But her father still lives at their old house. Maybe a new family will move into her split level house after her father moves out. No one knows where she moved to. If we find out, we'll print that information in our next newsletter.

Then Nikki thinks of the one about Calvin:

Thief strikes again! Ayanna Ford of Room Ten had her book money stolen this week. Everyone and all their stuff was searched. But the thief was tricky. He was able to hide the money probably at recess. The prime suspect has to be someone who has taken stuff from other people before. We don't want to accuse someone falsely, but prime suspects initials are C.V. We hope he gives the money back.

Uh-oh. Nikki swallows hard. She doesn't even want to think about how much trouble she and Deja are going to get into. She pictures her mother's wagging finger in her face. She sees Deja's aunt with her hands on her hips and her foot tapping while she waits for Deja to explain herself. What are they going to do?

"We're in for it," Nikki says at recess. She feels her lip quiver a little bit. "People are going to think we just made everything up."

"No, they won't," says Deja. "We'll just put the right information in the next newsletter. It'll be fine." Deja no longer seems very concerned. She looks like she is already scouting the yard for what she feels like playing.

After lunch, Ms. Shelby has them make get-well cards. It is fun, actually. It is always a special treat to have an unexpected art activity that cuts into instruction time. Plus, it is P.E. day. Math is cut down to only thirty minutes, which Nikki knows suits Deja just fine.

Nikki is still feeling a bit worried as she and Deja walk home from school.

"Let's do homework at my house," Deja says. "Auntie's home early today. We've got leftover pizza, and Auntie Dee lets me use the microwave, so we can eat pizza before we do our homework."

"Okay," Nikki says. Her mouth is already watering. "But I have to check in at my house first. I'll be right back."

Deja goes into her own house through the side door that leads into the kitchen. Nikki is back just as she's putting the plate with two slices on it into the microwave. Nikki watches with Deja as it goes around and around on the carousel. While they wait, Deja hums a little tune. Then, as if she just remembered, she goes to the sink to wash her hands.

"Here," Deja says, putting Nikki's slice on a paper towel.

"I'm really hungry," Nikki says.

Deja puts her own slice on a paper towel, then gets back to her tune while she carries it to the table.

"When we're done eating, let's play jacks," Nikki says. "On your porch. We haven't played in a while." Jacks is a game Auntie Dee insisted on teaching Nikki and Deja. They're the only two girls at school who know how to play.

"Okay by me," Deja agrees.

They are just about to dig in when Auntie Dee appears in the doorway. She has their newsletter in her hand, and her head is cocked strangely to the side. She isn't saying anything. She's just staring at Deja with an angry face.

"What have you girls done?" she says finally.

"Our newsletter?" Deja's voice is strong on the word "our," but "newsletter" comes out in a near whisper.

"Where'd you get this—this *news*?"

Deja doesn't answer. Nikki thinks there's something in her auntie's voice that's making her be super careful.

"We just got it from all around," Deja finally says.

Nikki looks from Deja to her aunt and back to Deja again, happy she isn't the one being questioned.

"I'm very disappointed." Auntie begins to read the headlines out loud. Coming out of her mouth with her angry voice, they do seem a tiny bit wild.

"'Bug Problem at the Denvers'? Overpriced Food at Simply Delicious Health Food Store?' I am so *embarrassed*." She stares at the document in her hand as if words have temporarily failed her. "And you have that little Antonia child moved away and now at a new school, when Jo

Markham, who baby-sits for them from time to time, told me Antonia's been in the hospital recovering from an operation. What's that about?"

Deja is busy studying a corner of the kitchen floor.

"I'm talking to you, young lady."

"We thought she moved away."

"When you're putting out information in a newsletter, you need to be sure you have the facts. You're not supposed to just guess at things," Auntie says.

"But we really did think Antonia moved, and we saw the bug truck in the Denvers' driveway, and I heard you say the food at Simply Delicious is way overpriced and you said Puerto Nuevo's food is swimming in grease—"

Deja stops because her auntie is holding up her hand in a way that seems to mean *Halt!*

"This is a problem. You two"—she looks toward Nikki, who is stunned into silence—"have insulted people and concerned yourselves with things that aren't your business."

This could go on and on, Nikki thinks, and now she's been pulled into the scolding when she'd hoped to remain on the outskirts. Nikki knows it's just a matter of time before Deja's auntie will be letting her own parents in on the problem.

"We're going to suspend this little newsletter

activity, after one final issue. And then you're going to go up to Puerto Nuevo and Simply Delicious"—Auntie Dee stops then, and Nikki wonders if it's because she kind of likes the owner of Simply Delicious, as Deja suspects—"and apologize for maligning their businesses. By the way, Keyon Denver works for Bugs Away. He probably stopped by his house for some reason. That bug mobile you saw in the Denver driveway is the one he drives."

Nikki looks down at her feet. Deja's auntie still isn't finished. She has more. "So your final newsletter will be one of retractions."

Retractions? Nikki thinks. *Is that anything like* extractions, *like when you go to the dentist?*

"And when did I give you permission to print out all those copies on my printer?"

Auntie Dee waits. She crosses her arms. Nikki waits as well, wondering how Deja is going to answer that one. But before she can, Auntie Dee hands the newsletter to Deja and says, "Get in my office and start working on retractions and apologies." There goes their game of jacks and the nice warm pizza still sitting on paper towels on the table.

"Auntie Dee?" Deja asks.

"What?"

"What are contractions?"

"*Re*tractions. It's like taking something back.

Saying that what you wrote wasn't true and then following that up with the truth. You'll figure it out. Now get going."

The girls get up and head for the door. Nikki looks back to see Deja's auntie wrapping the slices in plastic wrap and putting them away in the refrigerator.

10

Retractions

In Auntie Dee's office, Deja drops the newsletter on the desk. They both sit and stare at it. "Which one should we do first?" Nikki asks.

"I don't know."

"Let's do the bug one," Nikki suggests. "I think that'll be the easiest."

"'Kay," Deja mumbles.

Deja starts typing. When she finishes, the retraction reads:

> Oops! Guess what? The Fulton Street Newsy News Newsletter is happy to inform you that the Denver family don't really have a bug problem even though they had that bug van in their driveway. Their house is as clean as

Deja has brightened a bit. "Whatcha think,
Nikki?"

"That makes it seem like the newsletter made
the mistake and not us."

"That's what I wanted," Deja says, smiling
down at her creation.

"I don't know, Deja." Nikki feels a bit uneasy,
but she lets Deja continue to write the retractions. It's easier that way. Deja starts each one
with "Oops! Guess what?" It makes the retractions sound almost like good news.

Once they finish, they have to hand deliver
the newsletters to each house on both sides of
the block. They stand on Deja's porch and look
up their street and then down their street. "I
don't want to ring doorbells," Deja says.

"Me, neither."

"I know! We'll just quietly put them in the
mailboxes."

"Real quietly," Nikki adds.

They decide to stick together and take turns
tiptoeing up to the mailboxes. Each time they
manage to about-face and run with quick, quiet
steps back to the sidewalk, they both let out a
sigh of relief. Tomorrow they'll have to make
their trips to Simply Delicious and Puerto Nuevo

for face-to-face apologies. Nikki dreads having to do this. She knows there will be no getting out of it. Auntie Dee and her own parents will make sure of that.

When they're done, they head back toward their houses in silence. They reach Deja's porch and plop down on the swing with Bear. In the dying late afternoon, they can put off thinking about face-to-face apologies. Nikki decides to wait until morning to worry about that. But then after a moment she says, "I wish we didn't have to do those apologies tomorrow, face to face."

"Yeah," says Deja. "We're not going to be able to get out of it, either."

Across the street, Darnell's front door opens. Out he comes with his skateboard tucked under his arm. They watch him stroll to his garage, go inside, and then come out with two plastic crates. He lines them up in front of his house. Nikki and Deja exchange looks. "I betcha his mom isn't home," Deja says. There are no cars in the garage or driveway. Nikki has a feeling about what he is going to do.

In a leisurely way, Darnell gets on his board and glides down the block. When he is almost to the end, he stops and turns his board around. Then he begins to skate toward the crates, gaining speed as gets closer. Right before he reaches them, he does something with his feet, bends his body low, and sails over. Perfectly. He comes down with a small crash that sounds solid and right. He pumps his arm once, with his hand balled into a fist. "Yes!" they hear him exclaim. "*That's* how it should be done!"

Nikki and Deja sigh. "Shoot," Deja says. "I wish we could write about that."

"Me, too," Nikki says. "What would you write, Deja?"

Deja thinks a moment. "I'd write that while Darnell Woolsy's mom wasn't home—gone to the store or to the mall or something—Darnell snuck into the garage and got out his skateboard, even though he was on skateboard punishment. Then he did that same dangerous trick that he had his friend Evan Richardson do that caused Evan to break his arm. That's what I'd write."

Nikki considers this. "But we don't know if he's on punishment still. And we don't know that his mom isn't home. And that trick . . . maybe everybody does that trick and they don't even get hurt . . ." Nikki's voice trails off.

Deja doesn't say anything. Nikki wonders if Deja is annoyed that she corrected her. Finally Deja says, "I guess." That seems to be as far as she'll go. But Nikki knows that if they ever get a chance to do the newsletter again, she *and* Deja will both make sure to be real, real careful.

Because who'd want to have to do face-to-face apologies again?

They watch in silence as Darnell takes a second go at the flat-ground Ollie.

"Nikki," Deja says suddenly. "Look what I've got."

Deja is holding up the I Spy key chain. It's dangling from her thumb. She must have found it between the porch swing cushions.

"Oh, I was wondering where that was," Nikki says in a flat voice.

"Aren't you glad I found it?"

"I guess."

"You guess?" Deja says. "I thought it was such a great prize. The one everyone wanted and only *you* could capture with your special capturing trick."

Nikki raises her eyebrows and scrunches her mouth to the side. "Oh, yeah. Well, it got kind of boring, anyway."

"Can I have it?" Deja asks quickly.

"No. It's mine." Nikki takes it off Deja's thumb before Deja can get insistent. Nikki's tired of it, but she's still not ready to give it away.

"You girls hungry?" It's Auntie Dee, coming out to the front porch with two plates of pizza. There are two chocolate chip cookies on each plate as well. Nikki is surprised. Auntie Dee doesn't seem angry anymore. And pizza and

cookies together is not Auntie Dee's usual healthy fare.

Nikki and Deja eagerly take the plates out of Auntie Dee's hands and dig in. It's a perfect ending to a rough day. The next morning, when they'll have to do all that face-to-face unpleasantness, seems a long way away. Right now, they are just happy to be sitting here together on Deja's front porch, with their pizza and cookies and Bear on the swing, watching all the interesting happenings on Fulton Street.